T0327212

MISSIVES FROM THE GREEN CAMPAIGN

also by DAVID ARMSTRONG

Going Anywhere, *Leapfrog Press* (2014)
Reiterations, *New American Press* (2017)

MISSIVES FROM THE GREEN CAMPAIGN

DAVID ARMSTRONG

OMNIDAWN PUBLISHING
OAKLAND, CALIFORNIA
2017

Cover art by Vincent Valdez
from the series "Made Men," pastel/paper, 42 x 60 inches, 2004.
www.vincentvaldezart.com
@vincentvaldez77

Text set in Abadi MT Condensed Light and Garamond 3 LT Std

Cover and Interior Design by Sharon Zetter

Offset printed in the United States
by Edwards Brothers Malloy, Ann Arbor, Michigan
On 55# Glatfelter B18 Antique
Acid Free Archival Quality Recycled Paper

Library of Congress Cataloging-in-Publication Data

Names: Armstrong, David M., 1977- author.
Title: Missives from the green campaign / David Armstrong.
Description: Oakland, California : Omnidawn Publishing, 2017.
Identifiers: LCCN 2017020880 | ISBN 9781632430441 (paperback : alk. paper)
Classification: LCC PS3601.R5748 M57 2017 | DDC 813/.6--dc23
LC record available at https://lccn.loc.gov/2017020880

Published by Omnidawn Publishing, Oakland, California
www.omnidawn.com   (510) 237-5472   (800) 792-4957
10 9 8 7 6 5 4 3 2 1

ISBN: 978-1-63243-044-1

For Mom,
who taught me how to dream.

For Dad,
who taught me to work at it.

XX-78962

In the new century, it's terra cotta. It's ceramic.
Where is your home? they ask us.
In the earth, we respond.
And where is the earth?
In the clay, we say. *In the clay. In the clay.* Repeating it three times.
Planting the idea into ourselves.

At the barracks we sleep in long quonset huts, two rows of cots—
heads on the outside, feet on the inside—with an aisle down the center
and our footlockers lining the walkway. There is a small window to the
left of each bed. Each window is identical: twelve inches by twelve inches
of bullet-proof glass. A square foot of sunlight. Beneath each window is a
plant, a sprig of green more vibrant than any of our dusty scraps of pixel-
lated camouflage. Greener than even the ghillie suits worn by snipers that
make them look like sasquatches lying in the bush with their manmade
weapons of incredible accuracy.

The 'houseplants'—though no one here calls them that—beside
our beds are varied in species. They are given to us when we first step onto
base. Before we receive our uniforms, before we are shorn short, before
we're run ragged through the ringer, before we shed our fat or pack on
our pounds of specialized muscle, before our bodies become homogenized
limbs and heads and hearts, there is the Green Room.

The room is not actually green. Not actually a room either, but a
brick building with a single receiving door and a single exit.

First day, we shuffle off the bus. The sergeants greet us with invectives. Crossing the scorched asphalt we get our first taste of an unceasing hostility. The COs prod us with electric phrases meant to dismantle our individuality. This, they say, will become our saving grace. We're to be molded, kilned into hard men. By the time they insert our narrow asses into zones unknown, we'll know no environment is welcoming. You are never home. In all places react and adapt.

But when we pass through the doorway of the Green Room, all is quiet.

We're made to wait our turn. Along the right wall is a counter like in a cafeteria. Behind this counter stand five first sergeants. In front of each is a colored tray containing potted plants. The trays are orange, blue, yellow, black, and white. On the orange tray, neatly rowed, are areca palms, what some of the men call prairie grass. On the blue tray are young jade plants with their nubby leaves like rubberized baby spoons. The yellow tray contains spider plants, on the black, English ivy, and on the white peace lilies.

Almost no one chooses peace lilies. If you've done your homework you know, in the environments to which we're shipped, peace lilies are notoriously testy. The rest however are hardier, more durable and harder to kill, like good soldiers.

XX-91829

From my cot I watch the dawn etch a cold light across the window. It's the scraped gray sky of Patagonia in the winter. A photic line of ice on the pane prisms the light and caresses my hands, reveals me awake, my eyes unfocused.

I don't mean to weep.

Outside, in under an hour, the firing squad will tromp out and stand, breathing steam, in a field of merciless granite rubble. Flecks of quartz glinting in the morning sun. A halo of ground-born stars surrounding me in an alien terrain where no green will ever flourish. Is it really my fault? That a jade-green shoot of delicate and fibrous chlorophyl couldn't last? They'll fire and I'll be gone. Left to whatever seabirds breeze across the Horn in search of carrion on their way from the fishing grounds of the Atlantic to those of the Pacific, maybe even on their way back.

Yes, if the air stays chill, I'll feed them twice.

I couldn't have predicted this any more than I could have predicted Hershel Boyd. Hershel the fool. On the bus to basic he shook my hand. His palm was damp as a wet towel before a fine meal, his pale fingers long and dithering. He smiled in the way of men with too few friends and too great a need for them.

I took him for dimwitted because he spoke with a drawl somewhere between the viscous Carolinas and a light Kentucky cotillion. He said West Virginia, and I allowed he wasn't lying. He had a backwoodsiness to him that suggested rube. Then came an encyclopaedic spigot of babble, an unceasing brook of knowledge spilling forth from that kid's mouth. Passing an old factory for gas-burning automobiles, he mused aloud over the EU's climate ruling and their passing of an embargo against the US—"Then again," he said, "as Schopenhauer put it, 'Motivation is causality seen from within,' so what motivates the EU is just a series of disparate influences acting as a whole, am I right? You see the strings, and they all lead to parliament, right?"

I was having trouble righting the content of what he was saying with the twang in which he said it.

"Why what?" I said.

"Why we're going to South America. Why we'll be deployed."

"I don't follow."

But he'd already spun down a new topic, taking the factory's broken windows to point out that Spinoza, of whom Schopenhauer was critical, was a lens grinder and probably died of glass in his lungs, though the prognosis at the the time had been tuberculosis, a disease that also killed Modigliani, whose painting of Picasso was one of Hershel's favorites.

Maybe to catch up—his tangents made me dizzy—I asked him: "What's it going to be?"

"The green?"

"Big decision," I said. "Which one are you going to pick?"

"English ivy, no question. She's a natural in hardiness zones four through nine. That's a massive range. She'll go from juvenile to arborescent, grow up or down. I can back her up with cuttings. She does well in dry soil, keeps her leaves. She also evergreens through cold weather."

I tried to think of what considerations I'd made. I couldn't think of a single one. For lack of something intelligent to add, I said, "I would have taken you for a spider plant guy."

"Spider plant?" He made a comic *pfffft*. He played the air with his long index finger. He seemed to be drawing down some piece of long-stowed information. "Spider plant. The Mexicans call it mala madre," he said, "'bad mother.'"

A look of dreamlike sadness overtook his face. He lowered his hand.

"Why?" I said.

"What?"

"Why are they called 'bad mother'?"

He shook off whatever dream was haunting him. His flaccid smile slowly reshaped his lips. "They're also called airplane plants. They're for show-offs. I hope you're not thinking about taking one."

As a matter of fact I had. "You know shit about shit," I said. I became aware of a need to squash this boy, his hillbilly accent, his intelligence and enthusiasm. "Me, I think spider plants are the way to go. If you're ever going to be somebody."

He inspected his knees. "Why'd you join?"

"Kicked out of school a few years back," I said. "Had a job at the grainery, but there's no more grain. My checking reached two dollars and seventeen cents. That's when I was like, Sign me up!"

"Oh," he said.

"What?"

"Nothing."

"Why'd you join?"

"I'd rather not say."

I could see he was an idealist. One of the 'arbor specials.' Despite my first impressions, I knew now he was a rich kid, a private school kid with no idea the rest of us had to make a living.

"Typical," I said.

"What?"

Without having a clue what I meant by it, I said, "That's typical English ivy shit right there. Pumping a guy for information, no reciprocation. *That's* ivy."

XX-84554

At the end of that bus ride we crossed the lot and entered the Green Room.

Five men in front of me, I could see inside.

The sergeant didn't speak. He held up a firm hand. Sometimes he drove two fingers squarely and painfully into the chest of a new soldier who prematurely crossed the yellow line painted on the concrete floor. Few did. The Green Room was sacred. You took the cue, you knew your place, you shut the hell up. When the room was clear, the sergeant lowered his hand, gesturing for a new soldier to enter and make his choice. We were given fair time. If someone took too long, the sergeant tapped his foot. Taking more than a few seconds past that would have been an indiscretion to be paid back in sweat and blood during PT.

With only three soldiers ahead of me, I began to perspire heavily.

I watched as a recruit strode confidently to the jade plant and picked it up. I had the sense he'd come from a military family. Salute from the sergeant. Salute from the private.

The next was a sasquatchy-looking, big-footed kid, about six-four. He meandered over to the areca palms. The two of them, the soldier and the plant, wobbled slightly in the cross-breeze flowing through the open doors. He chose it and gave a limp salute.

Then just ahead of me, Hershel, confidently, his big nose aimed at his precious English ivy. Mid-stride a sudden hitch stopped him and he jerked. He half-turned toward the tray of spider plants. I could see it then, what I'd done. Hershel Boyd was a young man of a vivid and active

12

intelligence. Maybe because of that, he was susceptible to windshifts in conviction. He was "amenable," as my grandfather used to say about the men he'd convince to pay new-car prices for used. It's the same term he had used to describe my sister.

Pick the ivy, I thought. *Don't be an idiot.*

Hershel stared dumbly, his left foot cocked toward the spider plant, his right foot still pointed at the ivy.

No right choice. Variables all too great. But I did know this: you make a decision and stick to it. If not, you regret forever the moment of vacillation.

Hershel Boyd reached for the ivy. I exhaled. Relief.

Then he lunged left and snatched the small pot containing the spider plant as if he were stealing it. The sergeant behind the spider plant saluted. In his confusion, Hershel Boyd saluted the sergeant behind the ivy and hustled away.

XX-88960

I beat a boy half to death when I was sixteen. He was fifteen, scrawny, and a mouth. He said some shit to my sister. *About* my sister. It was the year before the Bicycle Law, and we were still being bussed to school.

As we arrived at the gravel lot the bell was ringing. I asked the boy if he wanted a cigarette. We slunk into an alcove where the kitchen staff smoked. I waited for him to take the cigarette and turn away to light it. I grabbed him at the base of his neck and shoved as hard as I could so his forehead struck the brick wall. What I remember is not the blood. What I remember is that I'd expected his hair to be greasy because it looked greasy. But his hair was dry, like straw.

The first blow nearly knocked him cold. Things might have been better for him if it had. I would have stopped most likely. Instead he fell and cursed me, dazed, and I fell on him and punched him until my vision went dark and only belatedly felt the thick arms of the cook and the janitor wrangling me away.

I was charged and expelled and never came back.

It's part of the reason I have no options today. The reason I chose the military.

For the record, I'd do it again. I'd do all of it again, along with all that happened after.

XX-85002

We no longer fight wars of desecration, but of preservation. This you will learn.
This you will know.

Despite what I'd told Hershel on the bus, at some point in the months leading up to my enlistment I must have made a decision. I must have weighed options, made little diagrams on scraps of paper detailing the most likely places I'd be deployed. I must have compared those with the requirements of each plant: accessibility to water, need for sunlight, temperature, adjustability to quickly shifting conditions. I must have at least eliminated this one or that one based on my own forgetfulness or even my overeagerness and tendency to over-hydrate.

Now though all I could think of was Hershel Boyd and the stupid English ivy he'd never have.

I felt like penance.

I cut hard to the white tray. A brilliant piece of plastic behind the dour-faced sergeant with the black hair, black skin, black moustache. Maybe it was the contrast of that vivid white tray to the sergeant's face and drab uniform. Or maybe it was the white-glazed pots of the peace lilies, so ridiculous in comparison to the others, which are all terra cotta, all matte and earthen tones.

Whatever it was, I've thought about that moment every one of my days in the unit. As blue shadows bloom on the land outside our barracks, I've thought, Why do penance with a peace lily?

XX-85743

A plant isn't meant to be held tightly, especially during vigorous movement. We call it 'leaf-rub,' the one side of a soldier's plant sheared of foliage from spending too much time against his ribs or back in the army-issued holster. Leaf-rub is the mark of a careless soldier, a man you don't want guarding camp on picket duty during the balls to 0800 watch.

Hershel Boyd was such a man.

Whatever veneer of confidence he'd exuded that first day had been based on the precept of choosing the English ivy. He'd read entire books about it. All the other options, including the spider plant, were mere background noise. And now he'd failed right out of the gate. He'd been deflated from the start. Not only was he unprepared for the spider plant's care, he showed little interest in learning.

I'm to blame for what happened then.

I, for one, should have recognized the early warning signs.

XX-88962

     I beat the boy because he'd spread a rumor. I watched each night as my sister wept into her pillow and asked our mother why people were so mean.

     My mother didn't have an answer.

     Two months after I'd broken open the skin on my knuckles on the boy's face, two months after I'd seen my last day in school, my sister slipped into a comfortable bath and turned the water pink.

     My sister was twelve.

XX-86641

You protect that which cannot protect itself. This you will learn. This you will know.

In the mess hall he loped toward me with his limp and defeated expression. His spider plant leaves lay in his spaghetti sauce.

"Don't let Top see you doing that," I said. I swiped his leaves out of his food.

"I fucked up," he said.

"Why'd you pick that damn thing?"

"I thought about what you said. I always play it too safe." He waggled his fingers in the leaves of the spider plant. It's a feathery plant and looks like it's tickling everything it touches. Some of the red sauce splattered across the table. I scooted away.

"Go with what you know," I said, repeating one of the phrases we'd heard our entire lives. "Not 'Try something new.'"

"Don't you think it's time to grow up?"

"I don't know what you're talking about."

"I just thought, you know, once. For once, I'm gonna grow a pair. Do something I didn't plan." He set the plant on the table away from the food. He positioned it like an interior decorator gauging the way the leaves splayed to either side.

Then he began to cry. I didn't notice at first. No sobbing. No tears. So maybe it wasn't crying. Just a snag of emotion which curled his face at the edges.

He turned to me. "What did I do?"

"You fucking joined the army," I said. "Now nut up or get the fuck away from me."

He wiped his dry cheeks. We were early at the table. No one else had come over, maybe sensing already a need to distance themselves.

"I don't want it," he said softly. "I've made a huge mistake. Do you think they'll let me—"

"Doesn't work like that. Get it together." I wanted to beat him within an inch of his life. I wanted to run. I wanted to protect him.

XX-REDACTED FROM OFFICIAL FILE

They smelled it on him, that sensitivity of spirit. They always do.

XX- REDACTED FROM OFFICIAL FILE

There is no hokey camaraderie with soldiers who choose the same green. All men, all plants are created equal. No spider plant buddies to watch his back. No one to coddle Hershel Boyd.

Basic went on.

A recruit named Sproat, the one I'd seen choose the jade plant, led the attacks. He always seemed to be there with his funhouse grin, his bared mob of teeth, under the watchful approval of superiors.

At night, after lights out, they held Hershel Boyd down and whipped him.

The NCOs crawled him across rubble, glass, and pavement. Hundreds of yards.

They shouted. They gave him special names they didn't call anyone else.

They pressed his face into the bed and jammed their fingers in his ass. They called him faggot. Sproat, often enough, performed this duty, telling Hershel he was looking for fertilizer and cackling with the abandon of a mad grackle.

They slapped his balls. They took shifts awaking him in the night, ensuring he was poorly rested.

They stuck him with pins, punched his kidneys, made his mates watch. I watched.

They pissed on him. 'Watering,' they called it.

They never touched the plant. I'll give them that. *Green stays clean.* That's another one they teach us. Doing anything to harm the green, even your own, is treason, the punishment death.

XX-87093

One day during basic, a fellow recruit, the tall boy named Dees, was scaling an earthen wall. On the other side of the wall was a dropoff, about fifteen feet, into a shallow trench of stagnant water. We were to hump up the slope, sling ourselves over, protect our plant, land in the chilling puddle, and crawl our way out of the muck to the next obstacle.

Dees did well until he reached the top. He hesitated, clearly worried about losing his areca palm. He leapt toward the water but in a moment of panic, tossed the areca clear, as if hoping to save it from being drenched. The toss went wild and, instead of landing in the soft earth, it struck one of the logs lining the course. The pot shattered.

Our drill sergeant blew his whistle. Progress was halted. The sergeant advanced on Dees, who'd frozen mid-scramble from the water. The sergeant straddled the areca, which lying there reminded me of a picture I'd seen once of an uprooted palm tree after the Family of Five—tropical cyclones Pyarr, Baaz, Fanoos, Mala and Mukda—emerged from the North Indian Ocean and trounced the coast, swallowing four million Bangladeshis.

The sergeant lowered himself to his haunches and carefully lifted the areca out of the sludge. It was still intact, but the cracked pot had severed some of the root system. I could see what looked like a chunk of scalp dangling free. The plants in those early days are so delicate.

The sergeant pulled his service pistol from his hip and pointed it at Dees' temple. He pulled the trigger. The metallic snick that hovered on the wind was more ominous than if he'd fired. It was a reminder, of course, to all of us that beyond these walls the chamber wouldn't be empty.

The sergeant sneered, made a motion with his pistol. Two MPs pulled Dees from the water. Everything stayed silent. Dees didn't scream, only held out his hands like a baby whose most precious toy is being left behind as his parents carry him away.

I thought of myself being pulled off that other boy who'd spread rumors about my sister, his face a smear of blood and broken bone.

XX-87051

I feel drawn to things that can't defend themselves, I guess.

Peace lilies are tender perennials, likely to perish in even a mild cold snap.

They require consistently moist soil. The soil should never dry out between waterings. You have to keep a watchful eye, is all I'm saying. You can't allow lilies to be on their own for too very long or they do something stupid like die.

XX-87149

I confronted Sproat one morning as he came from the bathroom
in nothing but a towel. He'd taken his plant into the shower with him, as
we were trained to do, but used far hotter water than was advisable. It was
a kind of showing off.

"You'll wilt that jade," I said, standing in the doorway so he
couldn't pass.

"Fuck off," he said.

I didn't move. Compared to the peace lily, the jade plant is a
thick-leaved brute, far more durable. If we were to tussle, he'd have the
upperhand.

"You ever kill someone?" I asked.

"Fuck off," he said again. His hyena mind spinning.

I lowered my voice to a whisper. "I have."

He lowered his eyes. I thought about telling him to lay off Boyd,
but it would have ended badly. I know. I was three years amongst jackals
before I traded them for this new set. I know what gets a reaction. I spat
into his plant. The soil looked positively artistic with my white loogie lying there like frog foam unabsorbed.

XX-87527

Know the EARTH, your future. This you will learn. This you will know.

Psychologists say the human mind has trouble processing the future as a tangible fact. Intellectually we grasp the aspects of the abstract, the possible contingencies of a world yet-to-be and never-to-be-revealed to us, but in our cold, reptilian need for survival we fail to grasp the importance of preserving our world for anything beyond our own physicality. We aren't developed enough to see the cells of our cells of our cells of our cells spiralling down through the generational helix, to grasp the big survival.

Like everything else we must be made to see, by imposition, by threat of violence. Via the military we are forced into conscientious consideration of the world around us. Of its future. For this we are grateful.

Hobbes once wrote:

The only way to erect a common power, as may be able to defend them from the invasion of foreigners, and the injuries of one another, and thereby to secure them in such sort as that by their own industry and by the fruits of the earth they may nourish themselves and live contentedly, is to convey all their power and strength upon one man, or upon one assembly of men, that may reduce all their wills, by plurality of voices, unto one will.

Hershel Boyd taught me that one. Showed it to me, and I wrote it down I thought it was so good. The weight of our will and the conscience of our people—our very survival—is borne by the treads of our modified T-72s and seen through the sights of our M-16s. It is proselytized with our heavy-slugs, which require less powder than those before us and kill all the same.

XX-87106

Beyond the training grounds the drill sergeant re-planted Dees' areca palm in a field of rich earth. All around it were the discarded plants of earlier washouts. Some of the plants had flourished—mostly ivies and palms. Others had browned and withered away. They were on their own. What happened happened.

We watched at parade rest from the edge of the field, each man holding his pot behind his back so that, from the sergeant's point of view as he rose and turned once again to face us, we must have looked very much like peacocks with delicate, green tailfeathers. The weight of those tailfeathers felt very heavy indeed. When I glanced at Hershel Boyd, who stood in front of me, his spider plant seemed to droop, to be on the verge of slipping from his fingers.

XX-77394

At the rehabilitation center, they were big on literature. Building cognitive empathy pathways, they called it. Rehabilitatable sociopathy, they called it, what we had. Big mouthfuls of words for a bunch of bad eggs. Patients instead of inmates, which always made me think of patience. Edmond Dantès. Sergeant Raymond Shaw.

Most of the guys didn't read a lick but still found ways of expressing themselves through writing—their own filth on the walls. I'm used to the grind, the cinder-block veneer of these places, white-washed but never clean. What most of those patients didn't seem to know, what most the doctors didn't seem to know, was that the books were bathed in blood. The ink is collated in a typeface that looks like tiny bodies lying next to one another, the serifs broken limbs torqued out of socket for the sake of style. I learned more from the page in the way of wolves than ever I did in the flesh.

Macbeth, for instance. Oh, Macbeth. Nothing but males. Smear the sleepy grooms with blood. I am in blood. So much blood in him.

The pages pulped of plant, but the words a never-ending gout of gore.

You can't stop us, I suppose, our horrors and our thirsts.

XX-87110

Near barracks, at twilight, I made out the silhouette of Hershel Boyd lumbering my way, his breath spent, arms slack, his plant bobbing ahead of him like a gift he meant to proffer up. He'd been made to run extra and to carry the green above his head. Before he reached me, he turned abruptly and headed toward a retaining wall that overlooked the repo depot. I could see what he meant to do.

I hustled out to him and spoke up just as he reached the railing. He held his terra cotta pot over the asphalt of the parking lot a good story below.

"You know what a stolon is?" I said.

He turned to me and scoffed. Hershel Boyd was a know-it-all. It was just one reason the others hated him. He couldn't resist countering with a factoid of his own.

"It's a runner," he said. "An adventitious root."

"Now you're just showing off. What the hell is an adven—"

"Adventitious," he said, swinging the plant inward, though not pulling it out of harm's way. "It means they don't branch off from the radical."

I played dumb. "Radical?"

"The regular root system. Don't they teach you anything in public school?" He stopped himself. "Sorry. That's my father. Always harping on public schools." He lost the thought somewhere in whatever storm was going on in that big head of his. For a moment I thought he'd forgotten about the plant in his hand, that he'd just drop it right there.

"They'll know," I said softly. "If you drop it, they'll know you did it on purpose. They'll make your life hell before you go. If they let you go."

He stared blankly. I could see in his drawn face he was exhausted, not just from the day, but from the past several weeks of torture. In the wan light he was skeletal, all concave apertures. His eyes were bright black beads in a skull.

"If you're going to do it," I said, "if you have to do it, make sure they see you do it. In broad daylight. Let them think you did it out of exhaustion and they ran you out."

When he spoke he chose to pretend I hadn't.

"An adventitious root branches off from the stem instead of the primary root system. It goes its own way."

He swung the plant toward me in a kind of about-face. He pointed at a slender, sickly shoot erupting from just above the soil. "They call these runners."

"Like a deserter?" I said.

"No," he said, regaining his former pedantic fussiness. "It's to help. The runners go off in search of other avenues of survival. Sometimes, like in the case of a potted plant, the root system is limited, so the generational survival of the plant depends on an outside means of reproduction. It's asexual, but it's necessary. That's why they call the spider plant mala madre. It's a bad mother. Her babies go off on their own. But they're doing it to make her proud, see?"

He pointed at the end of the runner where it had begun to hatch its own tiny version of the larger plant.

"It's trying its best. It's helping. The runner isn't pretty, but it'll reach out to soil beyond and find air and water. It's a necessary freethinker. It sometimes even makes a daughter plant or two."

"A daughter," I repeated, thinking of my sister, thinking of my mother who followed her the year after into the great, dark soil of an old hill strewn with tombstones at the edge of town.

"Did you know," Hershel said, "according to the Greeks, Pandora had a daughter?" He didn't wait for me to answer. "Pandora, the same woman who released all chaos onto the world, had a daughter. And that daughter was Pyrrha, and Pyrrha was the only woman to survive a world flood."

His eyes were nothing but flint-strikes, little flashes of reflection from the distant depot lights humming to life on the distant edge of the lot.

"Pyrrha was responsible for repopulating the earth after everything was wiped out. You know how she did it? By throwing stones over her shoulder." He made the motion. "Like seeds. This daughter of the woman who inflicted all the world with the worst imaginable evils was suddenly responsible for planting her offspring across the entire earth. Renewed life."

With that, he marched off toward the barracks. I wondered what he'd do. I wondered if I should stop him. Or maybe I'd misjudged. Maybe he'd never planned on throwing that plant over.

XX-87136

That night I could hear him turning in his cot next to mine. He whispered across the expanse. "My mother," he said. "She wasn't a kind woman." He giggled, his voice a soprano trill. My sister, God rest her, had laughed more like a man than Hershel Boyd. *"Mala madre,"* he said. "You know what she told me when I was eleven? She told me I'd better start thinking about the army because that bunch of tree-hugging faggots was about as close to a group of friends as I'd ever see."

I had no response for what he said.

"She sent me to live with my grandparents. Old horsestock people. Wealthy but in a hands-on way. The first spring I was there, I had a blast. I felt free. One day I was riding with my pap—my grandpa—on his tractor across a field. I sat on the wheel-guard behind him. They'd just harvested the winter wheat. Nothing but brown stubble. But you know what I saw?"

"What?" I said, despite myself.

"Green shoots. Slender stems. They were *so* beautiful. I just remember thinking, *I need to touch it.* I wanted to be close to the ground. I wanted to . . . to lie with it. That green. It was, I don't know, a compulsion."

"What happened?" I felt sick with his story, its momentum. Drawn toward awful inevitabilities.

"I jumped down," he said. "Nothing else in my head. Just, *I want to be on the ground with the plants.*" He chuckled. More high-pitched, more girly laughter. I heard him shift on his cot in the darkness, saw out of the corner of my eye the moon-grown obscurities of his rumpled blanket reforming.

"Too bad I didn't bother to tell pap I was hopping off. He ran right over me with the wagon trailing us. The wagon was loaded with a broken-down disc plow, massive thing, all metal. If it hadn't been for that, I might've been fine. Wagons aren't all that heavy. As it was, I snapped both tibia just below the knee."

Another airy laugh. "You know what? Lying there, waiting for my pap to notice he'd run me over, I had this weird sense of peace. Right in front of my face"—he raised his arm straight up into the air like a slender blue blade growing up out of his body—"there was that green little plant. I didn't know if it was a piece of wheat or a weed or some sapling lost on the wind and taken root in the middle of nowhere. I just knew it was beautiful. New and beautiful."

I rolled on my back.

"They understand blood," I said. "No matter what anyone says about the green, they only know blood. 'Go prick thy face and over-red thy fear, thy lily-livered boy.'"

I waited to see if he'd get the reference to my precious Macbeth.

He said nothing.

Hail liver, full of blood. The liver thought to be the seat of courage. To have a pale liver, the hue of a lily, was to be a coward. Macbeth, facing down ten thousand men, tells his servant boy to pinch his cheeks to appear as if he's ruddy with bravery—*over-red thy fear.*

That was one thing I'd learned of institutions.

"Blood," I said. "Green is nothing to the blood. You want to survive, pinch your goddamn cheeks."

"You chose a lily," he said. His voice had the distant quality of someone standing out beyond the living on the horizon of sleep.

After a very long time, after he'd stopped moving, I added in a whisper, "I chose the lily because it's poisonous. The lily. It's poisonous. Don't let them break you."

I don't know if he heard me.

35

XX-87139

I woke to Sproat screaming. Arms and legs jerking out of blankets, asprawl with life and alarum, recruits running barefoot across the cold floor.

I pushed through the bodies, Sproat still in his cot. A cold, hard turd lay on his stomach. An adventitious root cut cleanly from its bad mother stuck into the excrement like a candle on a chocolate birthday cake. Over Sproat's screams as he wriggled out of bed I heard the flutey, high trill of Hershel Boyd's laughter dancing on the air behind us.

XX-88200

Good, old American soil, they tell us.
In the clay, we respond.
Good, old American soil, they say.
Righteous soil, we say.
Wherever we go.
Good, old American soil. Hooah, hooah, hooah.

XX-88312

Sheer stubborness, I guess. That's what must have pushed Hershel through basic. Gumption, will, bravado, something boiling just beneath the surface of the flitty, pale-skinned boy. There were more beatings, beratings, and silent tortures, but he persevered, a runner sliding outward on a mission of survival.

XX-88698

Deployed.

XX-90291

The second time I killed a man, I was holding my peace lily to my breast like a newborn. We'd entered Argentina under orders, landing first on the southern coast of Chile before heading into the Patagonian wilderness.

We'd crossed en masse, two hundred men, on foot, no vehicles, northeast toward the interior; some savvy strategist's bright idea to invade and secure Paraguay's Mata Atlântica, a biome treasure cache, seventy-eight-point-seven inches of rain per year in the submontane and lowland tropics. Prime green. They'd never see us coming. But that was eighteen-hundred-miles to the north of our landing spot, nearly the entire spinal length of the Southern Andes. Not only that, but we found ourselves trekking the forbidden rockscape during the late winter, another major fuck-up, this one another strategist's failure to account for the southern hemisphere's seasonal inversion from our own. The seeming glut of vegetation that had welcomed us on our landing from the Pacific, once we crossed to the eastern side of the mountains all but disappeared except for the stingy, hard brush of the desert. For two days we tripped our way over a flat plain tangled in rocks and gray roots.

The going became brutal. Most of the men wore their plants tucked to their bodies bound in burlap to fend off sunscald and wind damage. If the terrain were especially difficult, we carried our plants under one arm, even though it meant being half as effective as fighting men.

We crossed what we could only guess was the nebulous and contested border between Chile and Argentina with no fanfare. Already we could sense we were in danger. Didn't matter what country it was. The landscape didn't magically transmogrify into green and golden hills of lush vegetation. It stayed the same or grew worse. We ascended in elevation, burning precious calories. We found only rock and patches of snow, jagged formations of million-year-old elements flexing out of the sea in a cordillera of inhospitable terrain. More scrub. Nothing but chaparral. More unyielding bark. No water. And no expert amongst us at extracting what the environment might hold.

Who had sent us here? Why were we being led by men who had no better knowledge of the terrain than we did?

I kept an eye on Hershel, moved between him and the others when it seemed they might try and pluck away his canteen. Our ranks had dissipated into clumps and in this way I found it easier to guard him against the others. Marching beside me one day, he whispered, "What are we doing here?"

"We're marching," I said.

"Where? Do they honestly think we'll make it to the Atlantic forest?"

"That's their plan."

"Do you know what's north of here, the way we're headed?"

I shook my head. His bookishness was no less tiresome out here in the wilderness.

"Petrified deserts," he said. "The steppe. Barren places that make this look like the Garden of Eden. I don't get it. It's like they want us to fail. Like they're testing us to see if we can survive. We're not going up to the snow or down to where water might have collected. We're in a no man's land."

The observation had a ring of truth to it. Would the army let us go uprepared to see what happened in real-world conditions? Was two hundred men a small price for an experiment? Were they testing the fallow conditions similar to those encroaching on all our once agriculturally viable farmland, to see what soldiers would do? I looked at the men, the boys, surrounding me. Were we meant to represent a cross-section of middle America?

"Don't let them hear you talk like that," I said.

"We'll all be dead within a few weeks," he said.

"Maybe sooner if you don't shut up."

"You have my back," he said, and sped up despite a now pronounced limp, compliments of his youthful injury.

XX-91445

Three weeks out we still hadn't found water beyond the scattered precipitation we collected in army-issue raincatchers, tarpaulin funnels attached to fifty-gallon porta-vessels. We were a non-engine unit, so the porta-vessels had become the only wheeled vehicles we could manage on this topography, four men taking turns pulling and pushing like kids with a wagon.

Emergency rations were implemented day twenty-nine. Grumblings circled camp that we were lost. Our superiors resisted trekking toward the white caps in the distance, telling us we'd already passed the point where hoofing toward snow and trying to stay warm would eliminate the last of our caloric stores. We'd simply go up, drink our fill, and freeze to death on empty bellies.

How, in this modern age, had we lost our capacity to bend nature to our will?

The soldiers developed wild and conspiratorial looks while sipping canteens, huddling with their plants and doling out the crystal liquid back and forth like two old prospectors sharing the last whisky out of a flask.

XX-91459

Day forty, things had become dire. Dehydration. Our faces wan. The whites of our eyes a jaundiced yellow. We traveled less each day. Deterioration is an avalanche. One man slipped and toppled from a loose path onto an escarpment twenty meters below. By the time we reached him, his lungs had taken the cue from his broken neck and stopped pumping air. I saw men use swatches of tarp to collect his blood and dribble it into the soil of their pots, hoping the plants would filter out the moisture so that they could keep the water for themselves. Our platoon leaders pretended not to have seen this. The soldier's plant they left in its debris of sharp clay like the talons of an extinct animal.

XX-91475

My peace lily had begun to thrive. I sensed it under the burlap
and confirmed it at dusk when I saw the brilliant white bloom, a small flag
of accusation. Should the others see, they'd assume I was stealing water.
If not executed, I too would be made to suffer an accident. I bundled the
lily up more tightly and kept it close throughout the day. Even when the
rainbow-colored motes began swimming into my vision, overlayed against
the backs of the men before me, I kept my lily hidden, safe, in the darkness near my heart.

XX-91801

Day fifty-two, First Sergeant requested volunteers to scout for nearby water. Most of us knew it for what it was: a chance to go off and die on our own.

Hershel Boyd raised a hand.

I was surprised. He'd continued to lag. The long marches and cold had seeped into his once shattered tibia, causing his limp to become prominent. I'd caught glimpses of him—ten or twenty men between us sometimes—slipping in the loose scree as we snaked across the untouched hills. I wondered sometimes if the man who'd died hadn't been pushed and if Hershel, if he were to stay with the group, might be next. I couldn't protect him every second.

Maybe those were Hershel's thoughts exactly. To die on his own terms.

XX-91805

I followed him into the wilderness.

Of course, I did.

It had almost been too quick, the call. I'd been tending to my lily, hiding it from the others who cast suspicious eyes my way. Nothing should flourish out here. Not now. In the midst of so colossal and vague a specter of death as deyhdration. We search for blame in the acute. We want targets but lack places to point our fingers and guns.

Sproat raised his hand to partner with Hershel. I could see the processes of his mind. The blood in him called out for more.

I stepped in front of Sproat and heard what sounded like a snarl at my back.

XX-91813

We'd been away from the group for two days.

Hershel seemed to be navigating with an internal compass. Sluggishly we scaled a bluff, going hand over hand until we reached a ridge strewn with more granite. Treacherous but it afforded a better view of the bleak valleys which scooped out hollows between the hills. We'd been staggering half-conscious since dawn, five hours, preserving energy, before Hershel spoke.

"I knew you'd come," he said.

"Might as well," I said. My tongue was swollen, and the words came out *mightathwell*. The air felt like sand in my throat. I formed the words with only the greatest concentration. How had I reached this point?

Hershel wheeled, surprisingly spry. "Let me see it." He pointed at the plant.

I could see he meant to go no further until I did. I peeled the burlap away. The lily's petal's edges had gone green it but was still an angelic white in the center.

"I don't understand," I said. "It's tropical. It shouldn't be doing well."

"They were getting suspicious," he said. "I knew you were next. That's why I volunteered."

The idea of Hershel looking out for me was absurd.

"I didn't steal water," I said.

"But you didn't skimp either."

"Of course I didn't skimp. I give what I'm supposed to give. From my own supply."

"Makes sense," he said. "You look worse than the others. Than me even. Most people sense their own survival being threatened, they cut back a little. But you. You're too stupid to try and survive."

He actually laughed, the high lilt again, though I was unsure how he managed it at all. Breathing to me felt like fire. "You're a perfect soldier," he said. "Somebody who doesn't question the reasons behind the reasons."

Was Hershel Boyd, of all people, at such a moment, making fun of me?

I said, "Better than asking so many questions that you can't tell your ass from your head."

"At least I bother to *look*. You're following what? Orders? Look around. It's all going. So long as we don't ask, it's inevitable."

I couldn't gather his meaning. My head was muzzy. My obliterated understanding lay in the corner of my mind, spent.

"At least I'll die with a good-looking plant," I said.

"No," Hershel said quietly. He made a grand gesture with his arm. "Not today."

Through the cleft of two descending slopes I could see the striking slit of lapis lazuli blue like a jewel set into the mountain. It lay beneath an escarpment capped white with snow. The water was unlike anything I'd ever seen. So blue and bright it hurt your eyes. More brilliant than a clear summer sky.

"Is that water?" I said stupidly. *Ithatwaader.*

"We're in the ablation zone. Glacial run-off. That's a lake." Then, because he couldn't help himself, "Silt comes off the glaciers and gets washed into the waiting pools. They call it rock flour. It's suspended in the water so it filters out some of the other wavelengths of color. What's left is what you see now. A gorgeous, opaque turquoise to the water."

It was like he were teaching a geology class or composing an ode.

"It's okay to drink?" I said. *Zogaydadring.*

"It's more than okay. It's probably going to save our lives and the lives of our entire unit."

XX-91816

We scrambled down the esker of loose rock, yipping and flinging ourselves recklessly, too recklessly for men in our state, toward that bold blue eye. We reached the bottom safely and stood before a meltwater pool of what looked like blown glass.

"It's okay," Hershel said, lowering to one knee to cup the water in his hand. His wrists glistened in a way that seemed alien.

So mesmerized was I that I didn't see the other man, not ten feet away, until he was pointing his pistol at Hershel's head.

In my haze my own service pistol was a bulky extension of my hand, the bullet a fingernail flown from the tip of my finger. It was as if I simply reached out and touched a spot beneath the man's left eye, leaving a hollow black hole in his cheek, and toppling him with one gentle push.

I stepped toward him insensate. The dead man was a member of the Mercosur Reserve. I could tell by the uniform. He was most likely an accountant or out-of-work retailer pressed into the service of that beleaguered unit, which was a tepid second to Argentina's nationally funded *Fuerzas Armadas.* He looked, fallen on his side, as if he were looking out over the surface of that fantastic lake. He looked hungry and dirty and battered like us.

"Do you think he was guarding it?" I said.

I turned to see Hershel on his knees frantically clawing at the rocks. His pot was miraculously still intact, but he'd dropped it. His spider plant and its soil had toppled out in one piece and crumbled in the rocks. The gentle water's edge had already pulled much of the earth away, turned it to particles too small for recovery. Hershel whined and dug uselessly at the stones.

"There's not enough," he said. "There's not enough."

I lifted his plant and returned it to its clay. Good old American soil gone. The plant sat very low, too low, in the pot.

XX-91940 (PARTIALLY REDACTED FROM OFFICIAL FILE)

Hershel Boyd is a hero.

Preserve this soil, preserve this life. For country, kin, and future.

This we all learn. This we all know.

Hershel Boyd is the savior of his unit. Slayer of the Argentinian resistance single-handed. We found the barracks, whose only custodian had apparently been the man I killed. There were rations apparently locked away that the man had not been able to retrieve. We managed to break them open, to find supplies shipped there perhaps decades earlier—blankets, pillows, heavy boots and down jackets no longer available in the States—and food of more recent deliveries, perhaps stockpiling. Maybe they'd expected our move. Maybe the man at the lake had been preparing the place. Maybe Mercosur Reserve meant to stop us from coming from the south as we had.

Our discovery was none too soon. An hour after finding the barracks, a polar cold snap clawed its way up out of Cape Horn, blistering the earth with ice, the moisture we'd prayed for now a deadly, diamond-like presence that jammed its way into doors, crept beneath our layers and sought to frost our skin, our plants, to bite off our fingers and leaves.

It was, in short, a miracle to have found shelter.

All because of Hershel Boyd.

XX-91817 (PARTIALLY REDACTED FROM OFFICIAL FILE)

Beside the dead man lay a small pot—much smaller than our own—containing a single cactus, an ugly, tumorous-looking green growth pitched in a tiny volume of sand, of no use to us. Crouching beside him, I took his gun from his hand and tossed it into the glacial lake. The big blue eye rippled gloriously.

I drank deep from the pool, my head in a state of dehydration-induced vertigo so I thought I'd topple right in and drown. I drank very long and thought very hard about what I meant to do next.

Sated, I sat in the rocks beside Hershel.

"Take it," I said.

"Take what?" He didn't look up at me.

"Take my earth. Lots of us can do that." I pointed at the corpse. "We don't need more of me."

"I could never do that," he said.

I couldn't tell if he meant killing or taking my earth.

He finally asked, "Why would you give it to me?"

"Always with the questions," I said. "You know that's the second man I've killed in my lifetime?"

He wouldn't look at the dead man.

"I killed the boy I thought was responsible for my sister's suicide. I'd already beaten him for spreading rumors about her, so when she killed herself, I found him and I stabbed him in the chest with a pocket knife too dull for the job. It was real work murdering another human being. I still see the blood sometimes. I spent three years in a juvenile detention center, five more to go, before a judge offered me a shortened sentence if I signed up to serve."

I unwrapped my lily and pulled it at the base out of the pot to show the soil beneath. The roots clung greedily to the black earth.

"I don't know that I could ever—"

"We no longer fight wars of desecration, but of preservation," I said, mimicking every CO who ever barked these words in our direction. *"This you will learn. This you will know."* I set down the lily and tossed a pebble into the pond just to see the water swell and lap at our feet. The miniature waves purled amid the rocks before knitting themselves back into a tranquil veneer. "I should have been looking after my sister instead of beating the kid I thought was responsible."

I could tell he wasn't going to fight me. He had too great a will to live. I waited.

Without looking up, he said, *"Macbeth* is a terrible play to quote. You know he dies in the end, right?"

Silence as I stared at Hershel Boyd. Then despite myself, I began to laugh.

Hershel Boyd laughed, too.

Our laughter echoed up the moraine to the bold, white expanse of the glacier above.

XX-UNFILED

In the army you agree to a transliteration of the old and dire warning, *If the plants die, we die.*

They have stayed my execution until the conclusion of the ice storm which buffets our newly seized barracks. The Patagonian sky, so blue before, has maintained a stultifyingly dismal palor.

They allow me to sleep with the rest of my unit because of Hershel. As he tells it, I warned him in time to slay the Argentinian. I am a minor hero to his epic. Two hundred men saved. Not only a good deed, but good press, confirmation of the rightness of our enterprise. Seems to me we're always looking for righteousness. But that's an old theme, one a soldier like myself is unequipped to question.

Hershel has assured me he's still thinking up loopholes. He's heard of reprieves, special circumstances. But I am a killer, nothing more. I accept my fate. In the new century a soldier must be a killer *and* a nurturer both. And the sudden death of my lily mere days after our finding the barracks confirms for many that I must have been stealing water out on the steppe, that I got what was coming to me by divine intervention. I have reaped what I must have sown.

Maybe they're right.

When the storm subsides they come for me. Only two of them. Sproat, who volunteered to be my executioner, and Hershel, given the honor of witness. Dawn, and they walk me out into the stones strewn with glittering quartz. A heavy fog still haunts us.

"We should go further out," Hershel says.

"Why?" Sproat says.

"Bad for morale. You don't want to look out the window and watch his corpse rotting day after day, do you?"

Sproat shrugs as if to say that would suit him. Still, he complies. Hershel, after all, is the new messiah in this unfamiliar desert of Sinai.

We walk for a very long time, Hershel prodding over and over again to go just a bit further, talking almost incessantly between.

"Did you know," he says to both of us as if we're on a nature hike, "*fagus* is Latin for 'beech tree,' particularly the beech trees of Europe. When explorers reached the southernmost parts of this hemisphere, they found what they recognized as beeches but not the kind they knew. They called these new beech trees *nothofagus.*"

"Nobody cares about beech trees," Sproat says.

"But did you know these beech trees, where they thrive is primarily in cold and arid climates like this one? Suggesting they've been around, been here, since an older age when the earth was actually cooler? Maybe an ice or two ago? So much older than us."

"I said I don't care," Sproat says.

"You haven't even asked what *nothofagus* means. If *fagus* means beech tree, then what do you think *nothofagus* means?"

"We're doing it here," Sproat says. He cocks his gun. I dare not turn around. I know he'd prefer to face me, see my fear before he fires. Staying turned away from him prolongs me.

"There are primarily two types of plant leading into the beech forest," Hershel says.

We're on a ridge like all the others. But now I see a forest of tortured green lying in a valley just below the veil of fog. Real trees. Maybe those beeches Hershel's been talking about. Real green is on the ground beneath them. And leading into it a carpet of smaller plants vibrant with life. Not only green, but red. The richest reds I've ever seen.

"Those two plants, the ones with the flowers," Hershel drones on, "are the chaura and the Chilean fire tree. Both blossom bright red. One might say 'over-red.'"

It's my cue.

I bolt.

There's been no pre-arranged signal. No plan. I only know it's time. That Hershel has relayed some message and I must act. My legs pump, my feet slide out from beneath me in a sprawl of scree and uneven crag, fissures, and chipped stones sharp as knives.

'Go prick thy face and over-red thy fear, thy lily-livered boy!' I think madly. And on the heels of that, *I'm a runner. A runner. A runner.*

They say you don't hear the bullet that kills you. It's already tearing through your nerve centers by the time the sound, trailing the slug which birthed it, catches up.

I hear a bullet crack the cold air.

Ahead of me are the blazing red blossoms of fire trees. The supple, bold berries of the chaura bushes. These berries, Hershel Boyd will tell me, are edible, sweeter than strawberries. "Like strawberry-flavored cereal," he'll say. "Like 'fake' strawberries." And he'll laugh.

"Nothofagus," he'll add. "It means *'fake* beech tree.' The Europeans had an idea of what a good beech tree looked like, but once they got to this strange new land, they didn't think beech trees here looked quite right. They didn't match. So they *must* be false. *Fakes."* He'll gesture to the trees surrounding us, the quiet green and the thriving plants in a new environment so unlike the one from which we came, maybe a vision of a whole world yet to come.

"They look real enough to me," he'll say. "These fakes. Just a different version of what we had in mind."

And again we'll laugh. We'll laugh to no longer be ourselves, to be free, to be surrounded by such strangeness and beauty.

DAVID ARMSTRONG is the author of the story collections *Going Anywhere* and *Reiterations*. His short fiction has appeared in *The Magazine of Fantasy & Science Fiction*, *Mississippi Review*, *Narrative Magazine*, *Iron Horse Literary Review*, *Best of Ohio Short Stories*, and elsewhere. His work has won, among other awards, the Mississippi Review Prize, Yemassee's William Richey Short Fiction Contest, the Orison Anthology Award, the New South Writing Contest, and *Jabberwock Review's* Prize for Fiction. He is a professor of creative writing at the University of the Incarnate Word in San Antonio, Texas, where he lives with his wife and son.

Missives from the Green Campaign
by David Armstrong

Cover art by Vincent Valdez
from the series "Made Men," pastel/paper, 42 x 60 inches, 2004.
www.vincentvaldezart.com

Text set in Abadi MT Condensed Light and Garamond 3 LT Std

Cover and interior design by Sharon Zetter

Offset printed in the United States
by Edwards Brothers Malloy, Ann Arbor, Michigan
On 55# Glatfelter B18 Antique
Acid Free Archival Quality Recycled Paper

Publication of this book was made possible in part by gifts from:
The Clorox Company
The New Place Fund
Robin & Curt Caton

Omnidawn Publishing
Oakland, California
2017

Rusty Morrison & Ken Keegan, senior editors & co-publishers
Gillian Olivia Blythe Hamel, managing editor
Cassandra Smith, poetry editor & book designer
Sharon Zetter, poetry editor, book designer & development officer
Avren Keating, poetry editor, fiction editor & marketing assistant
Liza Flum, poetry editor
Juliana Paslay, fiction editor
Gail Aronson, fiction editor
Trisha Peck, marketing assistant
Cameron Stuart, marketing assistant
Natalia Cinco, marketing assistant
Maria Kosiyanenko, marketing assistant
Emma Thomason, administrative assistant
SD Sumner, copyeditor
Kevin Peters, *OmniVerse* Lit Scene editor
Sara Burant, *OmniVerse* reviews editor